THE
UMBRELLA

BY JUDD PALMER

BAYEUX

THE UMBRELLA
© Copyright 2011 Bayeux Arts
119 Stratton Crescent SW,
Calgary, Canada T3H 1T7

www.bayeux.com
First paperback printing: February 2012

Cover and Book Design: PreMediaGlobal

The font used for the interior text is called handTIMES,
by Manuel Viergutz.

The font used for the cover text is called Diehl Deco,
by Apostrophic Labs.

Library and Archives Canada Cataloguing in Publication

Palmer, Judd, 1972–
    The umbrella / Judd Palmer.

Issued also in an electronic format.
ISBN 978-1-897411-34-6

    I. Title.

PS8581.A555U63 2011   jC813'.6   C2011-906578-9

Library and Archives Canada Cataloguing in Publication

Palmer, Judd, 1972–
    The umbrella [electronic resource] / Judd Palmer.

Electronic monograph in EPUB format.
Issued also in print format.
ISBN 978-1-897411-59-9

    I. Title.

PS8581.A555U63 2011a   jC813'.6   C2011-906579-7

Bayeux Arts, Inc. thanks the following for their continuing support -

Canada Council   Conseil des Arts
for the Arts   du Canada

Government
of Alberta

LIVRES CANADA BOOKS

Printed in Canada

para Mercedes,
porsupuesto

THE
UMBRELLA

There once was an
umbrella

3

who loved a man.

When the rain clouds raged

7

it sheltered him with its body;

9

and even though there
are many umbrellas in
the world,

and ever so many men,

13

this umbrella dreamt of
this man,

of how it would always
protect him

even though it knew

19

umbrellas are so fragile
in the wind.

21

One storm-struck day
there came a crow

23

who whispered: don't be
a fool.

A man does not love an
umbrella -

27

and as it flew away, a barbaric gust began to blow.

29

The umbrella was
wrenched from its
mooring,

and its poor frail limbs
were broken,

33

and its faithful hide was
tattered in the gale.

35

36

Cried the crow: let
thrum your heart to
thunder!

See how little that man
loves you,

39

now that you don't keep
him dry.

No, vowed the umbrella. I will not leave him -

and fell, unfeathered,
from the sky.

45

But the crow was
wrong:

48

the umbrella, though
broken, loved truly,

and true love is always
returned.

51

The end.